CC

LONDON CALLING

BACK IN YOUR ARMS

THE GREATEST LOVE

THE NINE LIVES OF GABRIELLE: FOR THREE, SHE STAYS

BOOK 1-3 COLLECTION

LAURA MARIANI

ABOUT THE AUTHOR

Laura Mariani is an Author, Speaker and Entrepreneur.

She started her consulting business after a successful career as Senior HR Director within global brands in FMCG, Retail, Media and Pharma.

Laura is incredibly passionate about helping other women to break through barriers limiting their personal and/or professional fulfilment.

Her best selling nonfiction *STOP IT! It is all in your head* and the *THINK, LOOK & ACT THE PART* series have been described as success and transformation 101.

She is a Fellow of the Chartered Institute of Personnel & Development (FCIPD), Fellow of the Australian Human Resources Institute (FAHRI), Fellow of the Institute of Leadership & Management (FInstLM), Member of the Society of Human Resources Management (SHRM) and Member of the Change Institute.

She is based in London, England with a strong penchant for travel and visiting new places.

She is a food lover, ballet fanatic, passionate about music, art, theatre. She likes painting and drawing (for self-expression not selling but hey, you never know…), tennis, rugby, and of course fashion (the Pope is Catholic after all).

www.thepeoplealchemist.com
@PeopleAlchemist
instagram.com/lauramariani_author

FICTION BY LAURA MARIANI

Gabrielle – from the diary of, is the first instalment and prologue to the series: **The Nine Lives of Gabrielle: For Three She Plays, Three She Strays and The Last Three She Stays.**

Yes, just like the nine lives of cats ;-).

The Nine Lives of Gabrielle Series : For Three She Plays, Three She Strays and The Last Three She Stays.

For Three She Plays - Book 1 - 3

The story continues with the next instalment when Gabrielle travels to New York: **For Three, She Plays.**

This is the first Trilogy.

For Three She Strays - Book 1 - 3

The adventure moves from New York to Paris with the next instalment: **For Three, She Strays.**

This is the second Trilogy.

All books in the three trilogies, including **For Three She Stays** are available individually, just if you only want to read one story and not the rest. These are the individual stories:

A New York Adventure

Troubled after the break-up of a long term relationship, Gabrielle sets out for a sabbatical in New York. A travelogue searching for self, pleasure and fun. And the Big Apple doesn't disappoint.

Searching for Goren

Why are we always choosing people who don't allow intimacy? Is it because deep down we don't want it?

Tasting Freedom

As her trip to New York comes to an end, her shackles bare falling and Gabrielle begins to taste, finally, freedom.

Paris Toujours Paris

They met in Paris. It was lust at first sight. It wasn't easy for him to feel this way. *"Dear Gabrielle: Don't be afraid of how much I desire you," Le P.D.G.* said to her in a note.

Me Myself and Us

Before meeting Le P.D.G., Gabrielle was a provincial middle-class girl who, against the odds, had made it in the oppressively male-dominated world.

He opened her up to sexual and emotional freedom she had never before experienced. But, despite his claims to her being the woman in his life, that did not imply she was the only one...

Freedom Over Me

Until meeting Le P.D.G, Gabrielle's experience of life was mainly secondhand, observed, and never viscerally involved.

Relationships aren't easy; they take a different take because of the memories and stories transformed during crucial moments.

London Calling

Gabrielle was away from the Paris office more and more, and working from home had started to creep in. From the London home.

London was calling, calling to write the next chapter of her story with him, and only him.

For Gabrielle had played, had strayed, and now she was ready to stay.

Back In Your Arms

"My darling, my love: I can't be clever or aloof with you: I adore you too much for that. You have no idea how detached I can be with people I don't hold dear. Or perhaps you do".

Gabrielle wrote to Mr Wonderful; putting words into paper seemed the only way to be fully back in his arms. After all, it was a letter that put a wedge between them.

"You have shattered my barriers. And I don't begrudge you for it …

I love you more than I ever believed I was capable of …".

The Greatest Love

With the death of her old self that she'd long been expecting and the birth of another, happier, higher one, Gabrielle stood erect and strong, drawing high and higher, until her stretched-out wings broke into fire.

She finally found a place to stand still, in love.

NON-FICTION BY LAURA MARIANI

London Calling

Calling

THE NINE LIVES OF GABRIELLE: FOR
THREE SHE STAYS - BOOK 1

LAURA MARIANI

To London, one of my three loves.
Shh, don't tell anyone: you are my favourite!

" TO CONQUER ONESELF IS THE BEST AND NOBLEST VICTORY;
TO BE VANQUISHED BY ONE'S OWN NATURE IS THE WORST
AND MOST IGNOBLE DEFEAT"

- PLATO

The crumpled piece of paper he was holding was not ordinary paper. It was a letter. A letter to Gabrielle. In French. He could feel somehow that his day was about to change.

Funny how things can alter so quickly.

The day had started so well. The sun filtering through the gap in the heavy curtains woke them gently.

His arms were still around her; he found that he couldn't quite sleep without being close to her, skin to skin. As if he was scared she was about to fly away.

Gabrielle was lying there, motionless, looking at him sweetly, her hair ruffled, cheeks flushed, trying not to breathe. Precious moments contemplating how lucky he was.

They were back home after a long weekend celebrating the day they met — he organised it as a surprise for her, together with an overnight stay at a central hotel. And then, they spent the previous day talking; well, for the first time, it was

Gabrielle talking. About herself and why she had been so distracted, he had noticed but was not going to say anything. He knew how difficult it was for her to open up. But open up, she did; it must have been excruciating.

"Good morning", she purred and sunk her face into his chest without looking into his eyes. He knew she had done enough sharing, at least for now, far more than she was used to, so he held her firmly, stroking her back whilst kissing her forehead.

"I love you", Mr Wonderful whispered, "always" he felt he needed to reassure her. He wanted Gabrielle to know she could tell him anything.

"I love you too, more than I can say", she replied.

Mr Wonderful believed she was telling the truth. Emotional intimacy was not her forte. She was used to standing on her own two feet and relying only on herself, not showing her emotions. But there was more to her, he could sense it, and he was willing to uncover the depth of her, bit by bit.

Gabrielle told him about her impromptu adventure in New York, travelling alone after the break up of a long-term relationship, and how she explored the city, spending time alone, getting to know herself.

. . .

"She also managed to have a quick relationship", he found himself snarking as he recalled the story about the VP, the places they had been and so on.

"Am I being judgemental here?" perhaps he was a bit; he felt a sting, particularly when she mentioned how they had met. It was almost the same as they did: a chance encounter in the street quickly turned into something more. He thought theirs was unique and magical; he had never felt that instant connection and attraction.

Mr Wonderful was sure Gabrielle had said something about never accepting invitations from strangers; it had never happened to her before either.

"Well, looks like it kind of had", he admitted, disappointed.

They had stayed in bed lingering—the crumpled bed sheets around them. Then, finally, Gabrielle got up and got ready for her morning walk. Mr Wonderful was a gym-type of person, and she was not. God knows he tried to organise sports activities and exercise routines they could do together. But no, Gabrielle doesn't do exercise. And that was OK; they both needed their space.

Between falling deeply in love and lockdown, they practically moved in together almost immediately, and he was wary of not 'overstepping' and being overfamiliar.

· · ·

He needed to do some work and thought he would ask if he could use her office; Gabrielle was precious with her space, house, and things. She wasn't used to sharing. He had grown up with four other brothers in Brooklyn, so alone time or space had never been a real option.

"Bye, see you later", she said, closing the door behind her.

Mr Wonderful jumped out of bed and into a quick shower before getting ready to do some work. He made himself some fresh coffee and then proceeded towards the small crook in the corner of the house that Gabrielle had designated as her office. In this creative hub, she did all her work, painting, writing and filming for her YouTube channel for her new creative career. The house had clear areas dedicated to different activities; she had perfectly mixed old and new, period and modern. Everything was neat in its place, with clear boundaries and multipurpose. A foldable antique lacquered screen concealed the area from plain view.

He sat down, powered up his laptop, checked his emails, and then the stock exchange, followed by a quick call to his broker to sell and buy some stock and shares. He had left New York a few years back, tired of the hypocrisy of the Upper East side scene and running around trying to avoid the paparazzi. Instead, he loved London, its history, the pomp and ceremony and, most importantly, the fact that nobody knew or cared who he was. He could pop into a bookshop, and nobody batted an eyelid.

. . .

He had been coming regularly to the UK for the British Grand Prix at Silverstone and tennis at Wimbledon, and now he had made it home. London had been calling, and he had answered. He was here to stay.

The desk was ideally situated by the window, looking over Canonbury Square and Canonbury Gardens, perfect for peace and quiet but also for people watching. However, he couldn't stop thinking about Gabrielle; he had never met anybody before who was this enchanting, enthralling, and so elusive. His previous long-term relationships had always played a second field to his business and personal interests: cars, racing, and flying. They simply couldn't hold his total attention. He had always been a very intense, single-minded person with a voracious sexual appetite and energy to spare. An all-or-nothing type of man and his all had not been love. Until now.

Now, all he wanted was Gabrielle. Her big brown eyes had captivated him from the first moment; her perfume seduced him, and her voice sealed the deal. But, most of all, it was her sweetness and vulnerability hiding behind the strong and badass facade. He had been careful not to scare her off with his intensity and had replaced his passion with old fashion romance and attentiveness in the hope of bringing down her barriers. He had acted like Prince Charming, trying to sweep her off her feet and win her over the old-fashioned way.

"Boy, I am in trouble," he felt it from the first time he saw her.

. . .

Mr Wonderful had been writing and checking emails for a while, but he now needed to print some documents. The printer was fully set up, but there wasn't enough paper for the file he needed to print.

"Where does she keep the paper for the printer?" he asked himself.

"Everything is so organised; it must be somewhere put neatly away. I am sure she has a place somewhere in here, hidden away from plain sight".

He started to open the drawers one by one. One quick peek at the time. He was surprised by what he found in some — a picture taken shortly after they had met — it seemed so far away, like they had been together for a lifetime and yet so close. Everything was fresh, romantic and unaffected by the lockdown and the humdrum of ordinary life. Notebook after notebook. One for every imaginable task and hurdles of sketching pads with all designs and illustrations for the new children's book. But no printing paper.

One after the other, he looked into them all and then, finally, he found it. It had to be in the last one, obviously.

He took out enough paper to cover his needs when he saw something stuck at the back. He bent slightly and felt his way through the back of the drawers with his hand to pull it out. The piece of paper seemed stuck in between, like it hadn't decided if it wanted to stay in the cabinet or come out. He was tempted to pull it out with force, but then he wasn't sure what it was, so he paid attention so as not to break it. When he finally managed to get it out, he realised it was a letter.

The handwriting pressed on the paper as if it had been written with haste or passion. He knew how private Gabrielle was and how long it had taken for her to open up. She only just told him about New York and her 'adventures' there.

So he left it be. Neatly resting on the desk. Mr Wonderful continued working for a while. But he couldn't concentrate; the letter was calling for him to open it. He was curious. He was tempted.

"A little peek", he thought", and then I put it right back where I found it".

"I shouldn't look", reminding himself how private she was.

"I wonder if it is something she thinks is lost? Maybe she'll be glad I found it", he said, trying to find a reason to go ahead.

That little piece of paper did not stop bating him; like a siren luring sailors to rocky shores, it kept calling and tempting him to open it and read it. For hours he resisted and kept on working, keeping busy. But he couldn't concentrate; he was too distracted.

· · ·

The letter kept popping into his mind. Then, finally, he gave in; he made another cup of coffee, sat down and unfolded the inviting note. And so he carefully, slowly unfolded the paper, a door to a secret world and started reading:

"Ma chérie Gabrielle, n'aie pas peur de combien je te désire".

"Brilliant! In French," how ironic "I find a new way in, and there is extra 'security'," he smiled.

Mr Wonderful French was rusty, but he could comprehend a few words here and there like "*désire*".

He understood it was a letter to Gabrielle rather than from Gabrielle and from someone who knew her, from what he remembered from his school days. Mr Wonderful glanced further, but his schoolboy French was essential, too basic to comprehend everything fully but enough to understand the gist of it.

He looked up Google Translate on his laptop and started typing the letter, line by line. For some reason, he was nervous. He typed word by word carefully. He wasn't quite sure he should. He shouldn't have. It would have been better if he hadn't.

But he did.

"Dear Gabrielle, don't be afraid of how much I desire you",

read the first line. He felt uncomfortable somehow; reading someone else's letter didn't feel right, even though he was curious.

"Who writes handwritten letters anymore?" he asked himself and cursed himself for not paying more attention to the French classes in school and not practising more French with Gabrielle.

The process of typing and translating phrase by phrase was excruciatingly painful. So slow.

I will shield you with love the next time I see you, with kisses and caresses.
  I want to dive with you in all the pleasures of the flesh so that you faint.

"Flesh ... faint. Who does he think he is?"

I want you .... to be astounded by me and admit .... that you have never dreamed of such things possible ...

"Astounded", he mocked.

... And then, when you are old, I want you to remember and tremble with pleasure when you think of me...

"Tremble with pleasure", he repeated "the man is trying hard, can't blame him for that", Mr Wonderful thought. Then, however, his heart started sinking a little, and his mind started playing games.

You make me hotter than hell ... everything you do gets me hotter than hell.

"Shit, very expressive" his throat was dry.

You have raised new hope and fun in me, and I love you, your pussy hair I felt with my fingers,

---

"What the f**k?" Mr Wonderful felt the words like daggers to his heart when it finally realised it wasn't a letter of unrequited love, a proposal ...

I felt the inside of your pussy, hot and wet with my fingers…

He had never swore or used explicit words with her, and she never looked comfortable when he played with her, always holding back. Always on the verge of orgasm but not quite letting go.

All this madness I asked of you, I know there is confusion in your silence — but there are no actual words to describe my great love….

My Wonderful had to stop; tears were streaming down his cheeks, blurring his vision. He hadn't cried since his mother died and couldn't remember a time he did before or after that, and he couldn't understand why now.

He stood up and went to make himself another cup of strong coffee. A needed distraction. A delay tactic. The kettle took what felt like ages to boil. Minutes went by like hours. He was pacing the small kitchen. Fear and anger replaced sadness and hurt, and then back again.

· · ·

He couldn't believe she was keeping this type of secret. She told him no more after their talk.

Shhhhh ... whiiiiiiieeee ...

The kettle, finally, whistled. Pouring the water slowly had little or no calming effect on him.

"Has she been seeing someone else? Is she still seeing someone else? Is she ending it?"

All sorts of scenarios were going through his head, and his fears and doubts completely overtook logic and common sense.

"No, can't be. She wouldn't have an affair. She couldn't have", he thought. "At least physically", reason starting to kick in, if only for a moment.

"Maybe it was before New York ..." recalling she had been vague about that relationship.

"No, it can't be. Gabrielle sounded peeved about it when she mentioned it, "Wouldn't have kept the letter for so long", Mr Wonderful concluded.

. . .

"Have they been talking? E-mailing? Face-timing? She must have". The running commentary in his head was driving him crazy with doubt.

Mr Wonderful sat at the desk again. The letter was there, waiting and bating him still.

Last night I dreamed about you; I do not know what occurred explicitly. What I do know is that we kept fusing into one another. I was you. You were me.

Then, we caught fire. I remember I was smothering the fire with my shirt. But you were a different, a shadow, as drawn with chalk, and you were lifeless, fading away from me.

Please don't leave me, my darling Gabrielle. I am nothing without you. xxx"

No signature, no name. It wasn't needed. She knew.

He read it and re-read it repeatedly, and then the translation. And again, and the translation. Checking he had typed each word correctly into Google.

"One of two words can change everything …."

· · ·

There was no date, and he hadn't found an envelope for it. But the letter was somehow 'lived'; there were marks, stains, and perhaps the slight tinge of her mascara...

He imagined her tears falling onto the paper and tried deciphering a timeline. But he couldn't, no matter how much he tried.

"She has a lot of meetings. She always takes phone calls in private. Was he at the 'meetings'?" His mind was now a runaway train.

Every time the phone rang, she seemed jumpy and took the calls away from him to another room. Her phone was always with her, texting and scrolling.

"Was she talking to him?"

Suddenly everything felt so confusing.

"Her aloofness was making sense now", he concluded, a sign he had disregarded.

"Where is she now? Did she go to meet him?" he couldn't help wondering.

"This is an awfully long walk", then thought.

. . .

"I should go back home now", Gabrielle was thinking simultaneously, but she was enjoying her stroll.

Gabrielle always loved walking and even more so during the various lockdowns, and now, with Mr Wonderful living with her, it was one way to carve some time for herself without hurting his feelings.

She always wanted an all-consuming, passionate kind of love, the 'you-can't-live-without-each-other' type, but she hadn't quite realised what it meant in practice, being in each other's pockets twenty-four seven. Or worse, intimacy.

So Mr Wonderful had his gym time, and Gabrielle had her walks.

She used to walk a lot by the seaside when she was little. The little village felt claustrophobic, but she always felt free by the ocean. Gabrielle loved the ocean, the sea, its temper, its moods, and the sheer grandeur. She always imagined the treasures hiding beneath, sunken ships bringing gold and jewels, people buried at sea and all the creatures who lived there. She loved watching the waves come to shore and the seagulls flying low.

Squawk, squawk ... squawk ...

. . .

She loved absorbing every bit of the sounds and the smell. So now she walked by the canal instead. She went there as much as she could. Watching the boats moving slowly, the seagulls passing by. It was her way to find peace and connect with whatever 'something' was out there.

Sometimes she took longer when she felt like she was losing herself. But one thing for sure: Gabrielle didn't want Mr Wonderful to feel she regretted moving in together or missed anything or anyone from her past. She didn't, really.

Gabrielle had permanently and firmly closed each door behind her. Her exes were totally and genuinely exes.

Only *Le PDG* had lingered longer than necessary. He had been contacting her from time to time, trying to win his way back in.

With him, she rediscovered her wilder, freer self, the passionate, inhibited side hidden for so long, her unquenched sexuality and her first orgasm, a part of herself that had been suitably reined in. But she had also found a part of herself she didn't like at all.

Gabrielle was scared now; she felt like a dormant and active volcano that may erupt at any time and cause dangerous earthquakes and mudslides.

. . .

Lockdowns had been a blessing in disguise for her when Gabrielle's healing journey began, and she stepped out of the craze of always seeking someone new and instead always meeting the same old sad, lonely child; herself. She knew she could not outrun. So she turned within and was happy for now with a gentler, more romantic love until she had found strength. Mr Wonderful was her knight in shining armour. Her Saviour.

"I wonder what Mr Wonderful is working on this morning? Stock, shares, buying a new company?" Gabrielle pondered.

She had fitted the corner of her house as an office/creative space since she had started her new career as a creative. All her drawings, mood boards, and manuscripts were neatly arranged in their place, ready for use but away from prying eyes.

Mr Wonderful had asked politely if he could use the space; he usually sits on the sofa with his laptop resting on his legs to check his emails and take calls.

She always felt that was her space, her creative 'cave'.

"What's wrong with that?" she thought. "I suppose when you live with someone, you need to share a little", trying to convince herself.

· · ·

Gabrielle wasn't used to sharing. An only child, she had only ever lived briefly with someone once before. And she never quite used to it. The sharing. Opening up.

"Time to go home", she said, returning to the townhouse in Canonbury Square.

Her neighbours were returning from their walk or whatever they'd been doing. They became 'close' during the lockdown, the whole square serving as an extended pretend bubble. Gabrielle had bought the house one year earlier, and she didn't know anybody really before the pandemic. But the community spirit kicked in on full blast during the pandemic, and in between the NHS clapping, they got to 'know' and support one another and even organised regular Friday night 'drink up' zoom calls with games. It was her place, the place she worked herself up to have for so long before events changed everything—Paris and then the big C. She could never bring herself to say the full word aloud, didn't want to speak it into existence even more, at least not in her existence.

Gabrielle turned the key and opened the door. She closed it behind her, slowly, still absorbed in her thoughts. She walked around the ground floor, but Mr Wonderful was nowhere to be seen.

"Perhaps he is still working upstairs", she thought. She could smell fresh coffee coming from the kitchen. She took a long breath in "*Sniff …. sniff …*' and inhaled '*Mmm …* '

. . .

She worked her way up the stairs to the corner study on the first floor. She was tired; it had been a draining few days. All that talking about herself was not something she was used to. Nevertheless, she felt she had to after the Opera. She had been absent-minded, with her memories taking her back and forward, shifting realities.

And Mr Wonderful had been so, of course, wonderful, thoughtful and caring. He deserved more.

And so, for the first time, Gabrielle told him about her solo adventure in New York, wandering the city, meeting the VP and their brief affair. Well, she glossed a little over the affair. She loved the idolised version of herself she could see reflecting in his eyes and didn't want to ruin it. Instead, Gabrielle wanted him to understand the sense of freedom she had experienced. Freedom and independence were important to her. Or at least the beginning of her freedom journey.

Gabrielle had omitted that she had also been running around New York searching for a fantasy figure, Goren. That would have sounded too crazy to understand. Stalking a TV character and his incarnation was too much to share and comprehend. Heck, she didn't understand it either.

Mr Wonderful listened patiently and attentively, asked a few questions here and there but was delicate enough to stop when he sensed she was uncomfortable.

"Thank God", she thought.

· · ·

Gabrielle was always uncomfortable sharing too much; if she didn't have to, she preferred not to.

She was feeling mentally and emotionally exhausted, but she loved him. Mr Wonderful was well and truly incredible. And patient. Always listening. Somehow she thought he was waiting for something ...

She knew she could tell him everything, and he wouldn't judge. Everything but Paris. Not Paris.

Mr Wonderful was a man of principle with a strong moral compass, and she was scared she'd loose him. His father had many affairs and left his mother to fetch for herself and five boys. This was one of those times when the entire story was better left unsaid.

"Where is he?" she wondered, going up the stairs.

She had created a little piece of heaven in the corner with her books, her YouTube set and the desk she inherited from her French grandmother. *Mamé* always encouraged her artistic tendencies. During her summer visits, they used to walk by the sea together and then stopped and painted. She wished she had spent more time with her in recent years. But, unfortunately, she was always too busy travelling. Working.

· · ·

"I'll go next month", she always told herself. But the 'next month' never came.

"Oh, there he is", she saw him sitting in front of the desk.

Mr Wonderful was slouching on the chair, a letter clenched in his hands, a throbbing wrinkle on his forehead. He looked pale. He lifted his head, and then she saw. His face was tinging on grey, his eyes red and swollen as if he had been crying.

He realised too he was not alone anymore. Gabrielle was back home and standing right there, in front of him, looking at him intensely with her big brown eyes, squinting a little. She was always doing that when she was thinking. Her cheeks were slightly flushed from her walk. Or perhaps they were flushed from the embarrassment of seeing him with the letter. Or guilt of being found out??!

"God, did it show he had been crying? Could she see?" He had wiped away the tears, but his eyes were still stinging.

He could feel his jaw tightening whilst his heart was beating faster, his palms sweaty. Gabrielle's hair was a little messy.

"What has she been doing?" imagining all sorts of things.

•   •   •

"What happened?" she thought. The way he looked at her sent shivers down her spine.

And then she saw the last drawer open. The drawer where she kept THE letter. The letter from *Le PDG*. Paris was still haunting her.

All her life, she had always taken the moral high ground on people having affairs, secretly disapproving of her friend Paola and her extra-marital sex on tap. A mix of her strict Catholic upbringing and *'le cadre'*, the ever-present rules with what's right and what's wrong clearly defined.

But in Paris, the lines blurred, and she found herself caged and chained to him, *Le PDG*, forgetting even common sense. And now Mr Wonderful had seen that letter.

"No, he didn't read it. He wouldn't".
    "Stupid, he has got it in his hands".

Gabrielle was trying to search through the chambers of her memory, but she couldn't remember how many or which of the lurid details were mentioned.

"But he doesn't speak French."

"Have you heard of Google, the internet, duh!"

. . .

"It's in the past; it's gone", she thought. "And how does he know that?" her alter ego intervened.

"Damn, I don't think there isn't a date in the letter", Gabrielle recalled.

"Oh God, he has been crying", she noticed. "He understands the letter ... "

"Does he think it's happening now???"

"What am I going to say? Should I say something?" thinking, thinking ...

"Perhaps I can pretend nothing happened; I haven't done anything. After all, I don't really know; something else might have happened".

"Yeah, right", the bitchy her alter ego dropped in.

"Wait, he hasn't said anything yet. No hello, no darling", she realised.

He was sitting there, motionless and speechless.

"What is he thinking? Is he going to say something?"

. . .

"Why isn't he screaming at me? Ask me something?"

The silence seemed to go on forever, every second steeped in fear and sweat.

Time stood still.

Neither moved. Neither said a word.

He was looking at her; she was looking at him for what seemed like an eternity.

Mr Wonderful wanted to ask Gabrielle so many questions.

"Who is he? When did it end? Has it ended? Why did she end it? Or thinking about ending it? What does he have that he doesn't?"

He had never seen Gabrielle's more carnal and sensual side, not the one transpiring from the letter, and he wondered why not. Maybe it was his fault.

"Have I been too chivalrous? Too Hallmark romantic?"

. . .

They had sex daily, but it was soft, gentle, tender, almost pure. Mr Wonderful realised he had put her on a pedestal, idolised her and had been too patient with her, making excuses for her, scared to lose her.

"Yes, he was going to ask her", he concluded.

"What if she said she was still seeing him somehow? What would he do?" he was sweating now.

The thought of not being with her made him feel sick. He couldn't stay, but he knew he couldn't leave either. So perhaps he should say nothing. Ask nothing for now. Wait for her to approach the subject if she ever did.

She was biting her lips nervously, which she did when pondering what bothered her.

"Is she about to say something? What if she is angry? Angry that he went through 'her stuff' and pried. He found something about her before she was ready to open up about it".

Her right hand was clenched around the strap of her handbag, her knuckles had turned white, and her right foot was slightly tapping. Mr Wonderful was looking for signs of what to do next.

Ring ring … ring ring …

. . .

His eyes flickered.

"Why isn't he answering his phone? Do something", she thought. He was looking at her.

"Oh wait, it's MY phone", she realised. Gabrielle searched for her mobile in her handbag, still draping from her shoulder.

"Why can't I ever find things quickly when I need them "... Lipstick, pens, notebook, sunglasses.

Ring ring …

"Where is the fr...ing phone?". There it is, at the bottom, of course.

"Hello Paola", she answered, looking at Mr Wonderful looking at her.

Gabrielle felt she had to make sure he knew who was calling. Just in case. The conversation went on for a couple of minutes.

. . .

"Let me check", she said. "Paola is asking if we'd like to go to dinner tonight, the last barbie of the season", she said, looking at Mr Wonderful. "Martin is cooking".

"Sure," he answered, surprising himself.

"What time do you want us there?" Gabrielle asked on the phone.

"Seven," she said with a questioning tone directed at Mr Wonderful. He nodded.

"OK, seven is good for us," she said to Paola. Gabrielle would have loved talking to her friend for longer, in private, but this was definitely not the right time.

In the end, she mustered up the courage to speak.

"Did you manage to do your work?" Gabrielle asked, her soft voice shaking.

"Yes, thank you", he replied faintly.

"Good walk?" he asked in return.

· · ·

"Yes, thank you. I'm going to jump in the shower", she followed.

"OK", he replied, and for the first time ever, he didn't mention jumping in the shower with her.

"I need to pop out," he added.

'Sure, I need to work anyway".

"OK".

Gabrielle turned and went into the bathroom to re-compose herself. She closed the door behind her and locked the door for the first time in a long time.

"God, I look like I feel", she said, scrutinising herself in the mirror.

She looked like a mess: her hair was all over the place, red-faced. And then she realised Mr Wonderful didn't stand to greet her, nor did he kiss her. He always kissed before she left the house or when they were going to be apart and when she came back, from anywhere. No matter how little or long she had been away.

"He didn't kiss me", she repeated to herself.

. . .

Finally, after what seemed like a lifetime, she came out of the shower: she had scrubbed so much that she looked like a tomato.

Gabrielle started re-composing herself and dressed up with her working loungewear, but she couldn't quite bring herself to come out of the bathroom.

She pressed her hand and ear against the door, trying to understand if he was still there. Gabrielle didn't hear him going out, and, right now, she couldn't hear a thing. Not a sound. She wasn't ready to be confronted and speak to him. Perhaps she could avoid him at least until it was time to go to Paola's. She didn't know what to say. There wasn't really much to say. *Le PDG* had been well and truly over for a year despite his attempts at reconciliation. Nevertheless, she realised that it was more than that.

Her ear was hurting now. She was pressing so hard. Not a squick. She finally decided it was time to go out and face the music. Gabrielle walked slowly, almost on tiptoes, turning around each corner with trepidation. Mr Wonderful had left the building. Suddenly she felt the need to rush to her desk.

"Where is the letter?"

There was no sign of it on the desk; she jam-slammed the drawer open. No, it was not there.

. . .

"Oh God, has he kept it?" she said. "He has kept it", she repeated over and over.

Le PDG wrote that letter to her when he feared Gabrielle was about to stop their affair and now was standing between her and the most amazingly perfect man she had ever met.

"How can I explain what *Le PDG* meant to me and why?" she wasn't even sure she knew herself to the full extent.

One thing was for sure. Gabrielle desperately wanted Mr Wonderful to know; he had to know there wasn't anybody else right now. And there hadn't been anybody else since him.

Beep beep beep …

A calendar notification.

"Sugar, I forgot" she had a zoom call scheduled with her virtual assistant to talk about her calendar, the cover for her new children's book and interviews for her podcast. It was precisely what she needed, some kind of activity not to think about what had just happened.

. . .

For the first time, she couldn't be bothered to put her 'face on' and decided to stay as she was, just reading her notes and preparing for the meeting. The call came and went.

Still hours before dinner at Paola's and no sign of Mr Wonderful.

"Perhaps it's better this way". At least for now.

Gabrielle reflected on how refreshed she felt after the New York sabbatical, with a new outlook on life; she had thoroughly worked on herself and done some introspection. Or at least was she capable of at the time.

She found out she had so many shields and layers that she struggled to penetrate them herself. She had caged herself in —a self-imposed cage.

All her life, she had been a closet bohemian. She always loved to live big, outrageously. Outside she was the perfect daughter and businesswoman but inside, she had always been Isadora Duncan. She wanted a life outside the bell curve and to suck the marrow out of life.

But she wanted people to like her too… And so she conformed. So much so that she had lost herself.

· · ·

And then Paris came. After the New York trip, it promised more freedom.

With *Le PDG*, Gabrielle became viscerally involved for the first time, a glimpse of herself. All the emotions, passion, her capacity for creative self-expression, and everything she had repressed for so long came to the surface together with their darker counterpart: jealousy, anger, frustration and obsession.

And in the process, she broke her values to meet her needs and got lost in the intensity of it.

Freedom was not freedom at all. Most importantly, she had deviated from her moral compass. Isadora or not.

But London started calling her back.

Ultimately, you can't run from yourself, but there is always one place you can just call home where you are at most peace and alive.

Gabrielle always loved London. Its anonymity, its modernity, the unconventional and the weird. History and avant-garde, tradition and modernness. The tolerance of religions and races. She missed the more relaxed lifestyle and multiculturalism London provides, the general politeness and lack of judgement, including sartorial standards. You could go out in pyjamas, nobody cares.

· · ·

London called her when she was younger and called her back when she needed it most.

Her stay in Paris concluded fairly uneventfully; Gabrielle started being away from the Paris office more and more, working from home. From the London home. Weekends were extended to Tuesdays and started on Thursdays.

The office didn't notice as she was usually travelling anyway. The only one who did was *Le PDG*. Their meetings became more and more infrequent. She just couldn't be in his presence. Their magnetism was far too strong and overpowering. She couldn't control herself when with him.

London was calling to write the next chapter of her life.

Then the pandemic happened, and luck struck to release her from his stronghold.

Gabrielle has played, has strayed and now she was ready to find herself again. She left her corporate job and started a new creative career that gave her an outlet for all the passion bubbling beneath the surface.

Still wary, though, of unleashing Isadora fully, scared of what she was capable of doing. At least for now.

She could see herself with him. She was ready.

. . .

"God, where has the afternoon gone?" she said, but there was still no sign of Mr Wonderful.

"Where is he?" She was both worried for him and panicking.

"What if he doesn't come back?"

They should really leave for Paola's soon.

"It will take some time to reach South London with rush hour traffic," she thought, looking at her watch. She was ready and waiting.

Mr Wonderful glanced at his watch.

"I should really go back", but he didn't feel like making the journey from Belgravia to Islington and then again to Richmond with Gabrielle, alone in the car, attempting to make small talk. Not right now.

He had spent the afternoon in his house in Eaton Square. He hadn't been there for months now.

He still remembered the thrill of buying the seven-bedroom, seven-bathroom Regency house from a disgraced hedge fund manager at a bargain price. Mr Wonderful loved the elegant garden squares and terraces of white stucco-fronted houses with pillared porches and black wrought-iron detailing, quintessentially English with quiet, traditional streets and a discreet feel. It was as if he had never left; the staff had kept it going as usual.

But today, the house felt cold. He was shivering.

He had kept the letter. Re-read it. Trying to rationalise. He was angry, most of all with himself.

He had showered, changed and gotten ready.

"I'm at mine. I'm going straight to Paola's from here. I'll wait for you outside so we can go in together," he texted.

Beep beep …

Gabrielle recognised the ringtone straight away. It was Mr Wonderful.

"What? Shit", reading the text. "At least he is coming and talking to me … kind of".

She ordered an Uber and waited. The car journey seemed longer than usual.

. . .

When the Uber stopped in front of Paola's, Mr Wonderful was just getting out of the car.

"Don't wait for me", he told his driver.

"Hi", she said.

"Hi," he replied.

He was wearing the silk navy blue shirt she bought for him with dark jeans. It made his blue eyes glisten more. She could smell *Dior Homme.*

Mr Wonderful had brought flowers for Paola, burnt coloured roses and sunflowers, and a couple of Martin's favourite bottles of red, Malbec.

"Thank God he did," Gabrielle thought; she had forgotten entirely.

Gabrielle was wearing his favourite dress; she hoped he noticed.

"You look nice", he said. He couldn't help it; she did.

. . .

"Thank you", she replied with a faint smile.

"Was this a sign?", she was pondering, but Paola appeared at the door before she could say anything.

"Ciao bellissimi", and hug them both.

"My favourites", she said, accepting the flowers from Mr Wonderful.

"Che bella camicia caro", Paola added.

"Thank you", flashing one of his dazzling smiles. "You look gorgeous as usual."

"Parole, parole … Venite, venite", welcoming them in.

Martin had reached the door too now. Mr Wonderful waited for Gabrielle to enter, holding the door for her.

"See Micio, that's how it is done", Paola pointed to her husband.

"Stop making me look bad," Martin said, laughing and greeting Mr Wonderful, the two men chatting away.

• • •

"Come, Gabri, help me with the salad", Paola said. "Let the boys look after the barbie."

"Sure".

"What's wrong?" she asked as soon as they were out of sight. Apparently, her face was an open book.

Gabrielle quickly went through the day's events, checking over her shoulder from time to time.

"Ciccia mia", and then Paola gave her a big hug. No, I told you so; no comments or recrimination—just a big warm hug.

"Let's have some fun tonight and see if we can oil things a bit," Paola said.

" LOVE ISN'T PERFECT;
IT ISN'T A FAIRYTALE OR A STORYBOOK AND
IT DOESN'T ALWAYS COME EASY.
LOVE IS OVERCOMING OBSTACLES, FACING CHALLENGES,
FIGHTING TO BE TOGETHER , HOLDING ON AND NEVER LETTING GO.
IT IS A SHORT WORD, EASY TO SPELL, DIFFICULT TO DEFINE,
AND IMPOSSIBLE TO LIVE WITHOUT.
LOVE IS WORK, BUT MOST OF ALL,
LOVE IS REALISING THAT EVERY HOUR, EVERY MINUTE,
EVERY SECOND OF IT WAS WORTH IT
BECAUSE YOU DID IT TOGETHER"

- UNKNOWN

THE NINE LIVES OF GABRIELLE: FOR
THREE SHE STAYS - BOOK 2

BACK IN YOUR *ARMS*

LAURA MARIANI

To all the lovers who are trying to find their way back

Mr Wonderful and Gabrielle arrived separately for dinner at Paola's house, a Georgian property, overlooking the duck pond situated in the quiet village of Ham, upstream of Richmond.

He was conscious of not embarrassing Gabrielle in front of her friends even though, most likely, he was sure the two women would speak about what had happened at some point.

But for tonight, he wanted to leave the events of the past twenty-four hours behind them and enjoy the evening. He liked them both, Paola and Martin.

"Interesting couple", he thought when he was first introduced to them.

A fiery Italian woman and a very, very Englishman couldn't have been more different if they tried. But they worked. Paola was a hot shot Chief Operating Officer for some global conglomerate, always travelling, and Martin, a Chief Financial Officer for a UK-based charity.

Gabrielle had known Paola for years through their work and had kept in touch ever since.

"Don't wait for me", he told his driver.

· · ·

"Hi", she said.

She greeted him as he got out of the car; she looked so good, wearing his favoured dress, and he secretly hoped it was for him. A gesture.

He, too, had made an effort and wore the shirt she had got him as a present and her favourite perfume.

"Hi," he replied.

Mr Wonderful had brought flowers for Paola, burnt coloured roses and sunflowers, and a couple of Martin's favourite bottles of red, Malbec. His secretary kept a record of all the people he met, personally and for business, and what they liked: places, events, and things and normally took care of everything.

But this, he remembered himself.

Everything to do with Gabrielle and what she cared about was indelibly impressed in his memory.

Paola was as welcoming and warm as usual, greeting them both with a hug.

"Ciao bellissimi", she said.

. . .

"My favourites", she said, accepting the flowers.
  "Che bella camicia caro", then added.

Martin was there too to welcome them.

As Mr Wonderful waited for Gabrielle to enter, holding the door for her, Paola jokingly said to her husband, "See Micio, that's how it is done".

"Stop making me look bad," Martin said, laughing and greeting Mr Wonderful, the two men chatting away.

Mr Wonderful and Gabrielle tried to act naturally, neither wanting to involve their friends in their trouble, both secretly wondering how the evening would pan out.

"Come, Gabri, come with me in the kitchen", Paola declared. "Let the boys look after the barbie outside."

Martin and Mr Wonderful went out and opened a couple of bottles of beer whilst getting ready for the barbecue. It was a nice but chilly evening, and the patio heater was switched on. They were eating on the open veranda, making the most of probably the last usable day of late autumn.

. . .

Paola knew there was something bubbling out and blurted out, "What's wrong?" as soon as they were out of sight, in the kitchen.

Gabrielle thought she had managed to hide the insecurity she was feeling right now but apparently, not. She recounted the day's events, checking over her shoulder from time to time.

Paola was boisterous and loud but knew exactly what to do and when "Ciccia mia", she said and then gave her a big hug. No, I told you so; no comments or recrimination—just a big warm hug.

"Let's have some fun tonight and see if we can oil things a bit," Paola said.

Paola put the flowers in a vase centre stage "Che belli", she said, smiling.

The table was overflowing with food: Italian assorted antipasti and prawn skewers, spatchcock chickens, coleslaw, salad, all washed down with plenty of wine, white and red.

The conversation was flowing, and they chit-chatted about all sorts of topics. Mr Wonderful and Gabrielle were sitting across each other, both furtively glancing from time to time at the other.

. . .

"Come and help me with the dessert Gabri," said Paola.

"Trouble in paradise?" Martin asked as the two women disappeared inside.

Mr Wonderful turned to look at Martin, surprised.

"Well, the two of you are always all touchy-feeling all the time, and tonight you are … hem .. just… 'friendly'. Is everything OK?"

He was about to answer when they heard, "Guys … shall we close the doors and move inside? It's getting cold now outside", Paola asked, peeking through.

They looked at each other, started moving things around to close the french doors, and turned off the patio heater outside.

Paola served the tiramisu and more wine in the sitting room where large colourful plump sofas were arranged to create a cosy and welcoming area. It was a place to slouch in comfort, English country shabby chic-like.

Tiramisu and more wine were followed by brandy, coffee, and more brandy until they all slouched and fell asleep.

· · ·

Gabrielle woke up, the first light of the morning caressing her face. Her head rested on Mr Wonderful's chest, his arm around her. She couldn't remember how they got that way but was glad they did.

She looked around and saw Martin sleeping on the armchair, his head tilted backwards, snoring with his mouth open. Paola was already up.

"Shhhh", she whispered, pointing at the two men still sleeping.

"What a night!"

"Thank you!"Gabrielle said, getting off the sofa.

"No problem ciccia", Paola said, rushing around and trying to get ready.

"I need to jump in the shower. I have an early meeting", she added softly. "You can use the spare bathroom if you want to shower", she added.

"No, it's ok. I need to go back home and change. I have an interview this morning," Gabrielle said whilst looking at Mr Wonderful, who was still asleep.

. . .

"Don't worry", Paola said, "Martin will look after him. Just text him."

Gabrielle nodded, picking up some of the glasses still on the table.

"What are you doing? Leave it, leave it. The boys can take care of it; Martin is off work today. Have you thought about what you are going to do?"

"Not yet", Gabrielle answered.

"Well, let me know if you need anything. Call me if you need to talk".

"Thank you," Gabrielle said as she hugged Paola on her way out of the house.

"Good morning, sunshine; how are you?" Martin asked as Mr Wonderful was waking up and stretching on the sofa. A couple of hours had passed since the two women left the house.

"Morning", he replied. "OK, I think. How much did we have to drink?" he asked while looking around.

· · ·

Martin waved his hand, pointing at the many empty bottles and glasses on the table "A lot", he said.

"The girls have gone out already", Martin added. "Both have meetings this morning," Martin said, reading a note from Paola, realising he was looking for Gabrielle.

Mr Wonderful checked his phone and saw a text from her:

> *I need to go back home and change. Have an interview this morning. See you back at the house later? G xx*

"Coffee?"

"I need a shower first," he said, holding his forehead "please," Mr Wonderful asked.

"Sure", Martin replied as he started collecting the empty bottles and glasses. "There are fresh towels in the spare bathroom you can use".

"Thank you. Let me give you a hand tidying up first".

After they both had showered and had some coffee, Martin said, "Let's go out for breakfast. We both need some fresh air".

. . .

"Want to talk?" he asked as they got out of the house.

There was a chill in the air; Mr Wonderful nodded, shivering, still wearing his silk shirt.

"Brrr … Let's go to this cafe," Martin declared "Too chilly to walk".

They sat down, and both ordered a full English. Somehow the boozing and abundance of food from the previous evening had made them both hungry.

"So, you want to talk about what's up?"

Mr Wonderful was reluctant to open up. Nonetheless, he needed to get everything off his chest and someone else's perspective, and so he proceeded to describe the previous day's events: finding the letter, reading it, his doubts about the relationship, Gabrielle coming back home and then hiding in the shower.

Martin listened attentively, and then he said with his English aplomb, "So nothing happened then …".

Mr Wonderful looked at him, surprised.

• • •

"I mean, you didn't have a fight. You didn't catch her "*in flagrante*" or something of the sort".

"Well, no. No," he protested.

"You just found a letter from a lover. Ok, a passionate lover, I'll give you that."

"Yes, but ..." when he heard the summary of the day so simply put by Martin, he felt silly.

"Have I been massively overreacting?" he thought.

"The letter could have been from a present lover, but how likely is that? You two have been together twenty-four seven since you met".

Mr Wonderful realised how stupid he had been when Martin asked, "What if she is? What if she is actually having an affair? What would you do?"

"I couldn't possibly stay ..."

"Do you love her?" he pressed.

"She is the love of my life", the words just came out of his mouth.

. . .

"Then, what's the problem?"

Mr Wonderful could not believe he had just heard that comment when suddenly Martin blurted out, "Paola is having an affair" he paused, "Well, regular sex with someone, to be specific".

"Paola is a very passionate woman", he continued. "I've never been 'that way' inclined. All I ever wanted was a companion, a family. She is an amazing mother and a good wife. We have a great life: she has her career , I have my family. And I could never leave my girls".

Mr Wonderful did not know what to say at this point. The man had a look of resigned acceptance on his face. He recognised that perhaps Martin needed to talk as much as he did, if not more.

"And you are ok with that?" he asked, realising he had a disbelieving look on his face when Martin responded, "Not exactly, but I have learnt to live with it. She is careful".

"Have the two of you talked about this?"

"Oh no, of course, not. She doesn't think I know. I found out by chance". He took a bite of his breakfast and a sip of tea. "A text. From him. He would meet her at the airport".

· · ·

Paola was travelling back to Italy every few months for a long weekend to visit her sickly mother, and then they would meet if it worked for both of them. Drinks, sex until the next time.

Mr Wonderful was speechless. He had contemplated what he'd do if it turned out that Gabrielle was indeed having an affair. He knew he wouldn't want to be without her. But the thought of another man kissing her, touching her, or worse, being inside her when they were intimate made his stomach churn.

"You have to decide what's more important to you. For me, it's my family. And I do love her. I know I cannot give her what she needs", Martin stated.

"I get YOUR point", Mr Wonderful said, sipping his strong coffee "But, you see, the woman described in the letter was not *my* Gabrielle; I didn't recognise her ..."

"And whose fault is that?" Martin interrupted.

Mr Wonderful was startled by the bluntness.

"She is a flesh and blood woman with her faults and failures. Flesh and blood, my friend. And you have put her on a pedestal, idolised her. You can't make passionate love to someone you are afraid to break; even I know that".

. . .

So simple, so painfully true.

The two men stayed for a while in that cafe, finding solace in each other's honesty for the first time in a long time. A new friendship was forged.

After a few hours had passed, Mr Wonderful made his way back to Eaton Square, to his house. He got changed, read some emails, and made a few calls.

He was dreading going back to Gabrielle's; he had made a big drama out of nothing perhaps and now wasn't sure how to approach it.

He still had many questions he wanted to ask her. He wanted to know about that Gabrielle she had withheld from him, was it his fault? Was he not satisfying her? But most of all, he needed to know if someone else was in her life now beside him.

Gabrielle was back home; the house was so empty without him. Although the previous evening felt like a step toward things getting back to normal, she knew there was still some mending to do.

She sat down at her desk, caressing the old cabinet, hoping her *Mamé* would give her some inspiration on what to do next.

. . .

"*Mamé*, what should I do? Speak to me", she said.

Gabrielle had always felt they had a special connection with her grandmother, and now that she had made her transition, she could feel her energy with her at the most difficult times.

"What can I do now?" she repeated.

And then it came to her: she should write to him.

Putting words into paper seemed the only way to be fully back in his arms at this point. After all, it was a letter that put a wedge between them. She had always been better at writing than speaking.

She took her notepad and started:

"*My darling, my love.*

I can't be clever or aloof with you: I adore you too much for that.

"Does this sound too 'writersish'?" she wondered. "I don't care. I'm going to write how I feel, no matter how it looks".

… You have no idea how detached I can be with people I don't hold dear.

She paused briefly …

Or perhaps you do. You have shattered my barriers.

"Is he going to think I'm unhappy about it?" she considered.

And I don't begrudge you for it.

She added, just in case.

There are not enough words to tell you what I feel.

It's a feeling I only get every time you're near, and I fear waking up from this dream.

The whole relationship had felt like a dream from the moment they met until now. A fairy tale, to be precise. She was the damsel in distress, and he was the knight in shining armour who rescued her. From herself.

Back in your arms is where I want to be. Once again.

Nothing ever feels so right as when you hold me tight with your arms wrapped around me.

She smiled, thinking about how Mr Wonderful could not fall asleep without holding her and how safe and secure he made her feel.

I nearly forgot what love was like until I met you.

Your first touch, first kiss, the first time you held me close.

"Mr Wonderful is a great kisser". She smiled whilst licking her lips gently. His kisses, a preview of passion simmering beneath the surface. She always wondered about that passion and why it hadn't fully erupted.

And as time passed, I knew you'd be my last.

I love you more than I ever believed I was capable of.

After the visceral experience with *Le PDG* she believed she had reached her full capacity for love. But since she had realised he was simply the catalyst to free a part of herself repressed for far too long that was dying to come out. And come out, it did, in a riotous muddled way crumpling all over everything. She hadn't learned how to control these feelings inside of her yet.

Gabrielle paused.

She knew she wasn't addressing the actual 'story': what happened, when and how.

"Do I need to?" Those details were irrelevant to her. She wanted him most of all to know about her feelings for him. However, she knew something needed to be said for both their sake.

You have seen a glimpse into a past long gone and forgotten ...

she wrote …

A past when I was still searching for myself.

You have shown me so much, more than you'll ever know. You have shown me the best of me, the higher me I had lost.

Gabrielle loved her reflection in his eyes, being worshipped and adored. He saw her as she aspired to be but was not quite there yet.

It is just impossible for me to say how grateful I am.

"Wait, this sounds bad. Cancel that".

~~grateful~~.

"No, I AM grateful. Very!"

.. truly grateful

, she added back.

You make me feel like I can fly.

No matter what she tried, he always encouraged her. Mr Wonderful made her feel empowered and powerful whilst, at the same time, protecting her.

I don't think you comprehend what you do to me because it's impossible to see. I never told you what I feel when you hold my hand.

Gabrielle could feel her stomach churning …

I've found my home in your arms, where I can finally learn to let go. I am still learning.

"Is it going to be enough?" she pondered.

In your arms, I am at ease; the world disappears, it is only you and I, and nothing else matters.

In your arms, I am free; I can be more than I ever thought possible and be stronger.

You cleaned up the mess and healed my wounds, and now I'm beginning to be whole again.

Gabrielle had felt 'unclean' after Paris.

Even though she always had a very liberal view of sex and relationships, she had always drawn the line to getting involved with men who had any type of commitment. And in Paris, she perpetrated the ultimate sin; an affair with a married man. She remembered how she felt when she had been cheated on.

The anger. The disgust.

Still, it was as if she had an extra-corporeal experience. As if someone else had an affair, not her. She was ashamed. The only thing she had been missing was the more carnal part of herself that she had rediscovered and now had put on hold again. At least until she knew how to control and channel it in a more positive way,

---

In your arms, I've found my purpose, and there's nothing I can't do, no limits I can't transcend.

In your arms, anything is possible.

In your arms, I find safety like no other, and I can breathe deep, knowing you'll always keep me close and never hurt me.

So please, my darling, hold me close, don't let me go.
    My heart belongs to you. This you must know.
    I want to be here with you, not only for today but forever in your arms stay.

In your arms, I am home".

Now that she had put her heart to paper, Gabrielle relaxed in the chair.

drip, drop … , slap, slash, splash … rat-a-tat-tat

It had started to rain, the drops splattering against the window. She sat there re-reading what she had written and thinking if she should type it but decided against it and copied her words in full into her monogrammed letter sheets.

· · ·

Handwritten.

It was getting dark. She folded the letter neatly into an envelope, wrote his name across it, and then left it on the desk.

Mr Wonderful was not back home yet. Gabrielle was debating whether to wait for him or to go out: she had to pop out to pick up some dry cleaning she needed the next day and some groceries. She still hadn't figured out how to approach the subject when she saw him: what to say, how to say, how to hand him the letter.

She looked at her watch "The dry cleaner will be closing soon; I need to go", she decided.

Mr Wonderful looked at his watch, "It is time to go back to Gabrielle's", he thought.

He called the driver to get the car ready in five minutes while he popped to the florist next door. "Gabrielle loves flowers".

"A dozen pink roses", he said to the florist. An apology bouquet.

The driver dropped him off at the Islington Townhouse. Somehow he felt more at home there than in his own house. Wherever she was, it was home for him.

.   .   .

"Gabri", he called out as he entered the house.

There was no one there.

He looked around, but she was not in. He walked up the stairs where the whole kerfuffle started. And there it was; a closed envelope with his name on the bare desk.

He sat down on the same chair where twenty-four hours earlier, found the other letter. This time though, he opened the envelope with a feeling of anticipation, unfolded the hand-written letter and began to read:

"My darling, my love…

He read slowly, soaking in every word.

… I nearly forgot what love was like until I met you.

He read and re-read it and dissected every word.

You have seen a glimpse into a past long gone and forgotten. A past when I was still searching for myself.

Gabrielle had not really talked about what had happened, but whatever it was, it was now over. In his heart of heart, he believed it.

As Mr Wonderful looked up, he saw her: Gabrielle was standing in front of him, looking nervous.

It had only been a day, but he had missed holding her, kissing her.

He stood up and walked towards her. Tears were falling down her cheeks.

"I love you", she said.

"I love you too", he replied.

And then she was back in his arms where she belonged.

THE NINE LIVES OF GABRIELLE:
FOR THREE SHE STAYS - BOOK 3

The
Greatest
Love

LAURA MARIANI

I hope you all find what you are looking for

Your task is not to seek for LOVE,
but merely to seek and find all the barriers within yourself
that you have built against it

Rumi

"My darling, my love,

I can't be clever or aloof with you: I adore you too much for that.

You have no idea how detached I can be with people I don't hold dear. Or perhaps you do.

You have shattered my barriers. And I don't begrudge you for it.

There are not enough words to tell you what I feel,
It's a feeling I only get every time you're near, and I fear waking from this dream.

Back in your arms is where I want to be once again.
Nothing ever feels so right as when you hold me tight with your arms wrapped around me.

I nearly forgot what love was like until I met you.
Your first touch, first kiss, the first time you held me close.
And as time passed, I knew you'd be my last.
I love you more than I ever believed I was capable of.

You have seen a glimpse into a past long gone and forgotten—
a past when I was still searching for myself.

You have shown me so much, more than you'll ever know. You have shown me the best of me, the higher me I had lost.

It is just impossible for me to say how truly grateful I am.

You make me feel like I can fly.

I don't think you comprehend what you do to me because it's impossible to see. I never told you what I feel when you hold my hand.

I've found my home in your arms, where I can finally learn to let go.

In your arms, I am at ease; the world disappears until it is only you and I, and nothing else matters.

In your arms, I am free; I can be more than I ever thought possible and be stronger.

You cleaned up the mess and healed my wounds, and now I'm beginning to be whole again.

In your arms, I've found my purpose, and there's nothing I can't do, no limits I can't transcend.
  In your arms, anything is possible.

In your arms, I find safety like no other, and I can breathe deep, knowing you'll always keep me close and never hurt me.

So please, my darling, hold me close, don't let me go.
  My heart belongs to you. This you must know.

I want to be here with you, not only for today but forever in your arms stay.

In your arms, I am home".

D ays had gone by since he had first read it. Mr Wonderful had kept Gabrielle's handwritten note neatly folded in his wallet, the only single reminder of the events. Life had continued unchanged since then.

He was, of course, happy: he could not envision a life without her. But Martin's comments were playing in his head nonstop.

"And whose fault is that?" Martin had said. "She is a flesh and blood woman with her faults and failures. Flesh and blood, my friend".

"Yes, she was", he had discovered in the letter from her ex-lover, "fresh and blood, sweat and tears. He had never seen 'That' Gabrielle", he thought.

"And you have put her on a pedestal, idolised her. You can't make passionate love to someone you are afraid to break; even I know that" Martin had noted.

He was right: Mr Wonderful was afraid to lose and break her; he had idolised her.

"You have shown me the best of me, the higher me I had lost". Gabrielle had written.

And she was *"truly grateful"* for it, he recalled.

. . .

This exalted but fragile version of Gabrielle in his head did not allow him to love her with the unbridled passion he was capable of and to satisfy his needs, nor enable her to be herself. Fully.

"Would he have reacted in the same way to the letter had he not thought of her that way?" the thought mulling in his head repeatedly.

"Probably not", he concluded. His expectations of her and himself were perhaps romantic of a bygone era.

He loved her for what he could see she was underneath her protective shield, and he wanted to protect her.

He loved her for he could be when he was with her.

Deep down in his heart, he knew they both needed to become more 'human'.

Both were enamoured with the idealised version of self when they were together.

"You have shown me the best of me, the higher me I had lost", … *drum drum* drumming in his head …

. . .

… *"In your arms, I find safety like no other, and I can breathe deep, knowing you'll always keep me close and never hurt me".*

"Safe", he thought, "she feels safe", he repeated.

He knew he always wanted her to feel secure, but not *just* so. He desired to satisfy her deepest needs and wants. ALL of her needs. And his own.

He had lived a very driven, passionate visceral life in every area before, except love, and he wanted that. Needed it. And now he could no longer ignore that; he knew neither could she.

… *"You cleaned up the mess and healed my wounds, and now I'm beginning to be whole again",* *…* *drum drum.*

Something was stopping her, though, and she was not ready to talk about it.

He had noticed that Gabrielle had been particularly caring with him and more demonstrative than usual. He did not know how to encourage her to let go and let him in, if only a little more.

Mr Wonderful folded back the note and put it in his wallet.

· · ·

"Time", he said. "It will take time", he repeated to convince himself.

Gabrielle was content that things were back to normal. Mr Wonderful was as chivalrous as usual and had not asked any more questions about the infamous letter.

He looked genuinely surprised and pleased she wrote to him and expressed her feelings.

"It wasn't as painful as I expected", she thought. "I should do it more often", she professed.

But life took over, and she forgot her pledge. Time passed by.

Mr Wonderful, however, wanted to know more, increasingly so. He realised that if he didn't push and prod, she wouldn't volunteer more insights into her past life or soul, for that matter.

"How long was the relationship?" he asked one day.

He knew it had ended but wished to learn more.

"It must have been significant, or she wouldn't have kept that letter".

. . .

"Why has it been so painful?" he couldn't figure it out.

"Why was she holding on and not abandoning herself to sheer pleasure when they were making love?"

One afternoon he had walked in on her as she was pleasuring herself. He stood there and watched silently, unknown to her. He witnessed her sheer abandonment of the flesh and joy in the act. Her face transfixed, her voice raucous.

He watched her touching herself aptly, knowing how to take it slowly or come quickly several times. But not with him. He was beginning to think it WAS him.

Gabrielle always seemed to squirm uncomfortably under his questions, glossing over her answer and changing subject swiftly.

Mr Wonderful knew he wanted more now. She was capable of more.

He tried to emulate what he had seen her doing.

He touched how she touched herself. He touched her where she touched herself.

. . .

But Gabrielle always managed to hold back to the point that he was sure she was faking orgasm 'to get it over with'.

"He deserved more", he thought.

And it wasn't just about sex, although he felt the need for a more visceral experience. It was about intimacy, the ability and willingness to be vulnerable with each other. And trust.

He had told her about his family, his abusive and philandering father who abandoned his mother and four other brothers, their struggle for a long time and how he made his fortune.

She knew his whole life story. He had been delicate about the details of his past relationships, although most of them had been played out in the press and were common knowledge, at least the gossip. Nevertheless, he had not kept anything from her and had answered any questions she asked.

Sometimes she seemed curious, and he was pleased she was showing an interest. But was not willing or able to do so herself.

Mr Wonderful had lived with Gabrielle in her Islington townhouse and realised she had never even spent the night at his.

. . .

He had given her a set of keys and made space in his wardrobe for her. Although he didn't necessarily want to move back or live in Belgravia, he wished she at least tried.

He hoped she did.
    He wanted her to.
    He waited for her to.

Time went by.

Gabrielle returned home from doing some errands to find a set of luggage by the front door. She didn't recognise them.

"Perhaps Mr Wonderful had planned a surprise getaway together?" she thought excitedly.

"Darling?" she called. She looked around and found him upstairs, sitting at her desk with his coat on.

"Hi", she said.

When he looked up, she realised something was wrong.

Mr Wonderful never thought he would ever come to this, saying goodbye.

·   ·   ·

Gabrielle was staring at him, looking fearful.

"My darling," he said. "I think it would be better if we take a break for a while."

Gabrielle looked at him incredulously; she could not believe he was saying that. Tears started falling down her cheeks.

"We can't …."

"Why can't we be together?" she interrupted, weeping.

She was desperate to know why he had to say goodbye. "Surely not; I have misheard him".

She was desperate for him to answer why they couldn't be together.

They loved each other, didn't they?

"I will always love you", he continued.

He got closer to her and then held her face in his hands while looking into those big brown eyes he fell in love with. He slowly patted her tears dry, trying to be strong for both of them. But it was hard, more difficult than he had imagined, and he couldn't control himself.

. . .

He held her a bit longer and told her he would wait for her.

"My darling, your wounds are still open, and you are the only one who can truly heal them and make yourself whole. Be comfortable with every part of you and what you need and want".

Gabrielle couldn't grasp what he was saying.

"You shouldn't be scared of yourself and what you can be. But my darling, please do know that no matter how long it will take, if you still want me, Io ti aspetto".

She was confused. Soon he told her he would be able to hold her tight and never have to let go again, she heard.

Soon.

But the pain of saying goodbye was too much right now.

"Don't cry," he uttered with tears in his eyes.

'How long am I going to be without you?" she whispered to him.
   "How long?" she said, sobbing. "Please tell me".

·   ·   ·

"Don't forget me", he added, unsure how to answer.

"How could I ever?" she thought.

"I could never live my life fully without you," she said, unable to hold back her emotions, "You are the best part of me", and more tears started pouring down her cheeks.

"Let's make a date", he then declared. He was too scared, leaving it open-ended. He needed a date to look forward to.

"Let's meet on top of the Empire State Building", he proposed hopeful. They had watched *An Affair to Remember* many times together, and both loved how sweepingly romantic it was.

Gabrielle smiled through her tears, nodding.

"Six months from today", he was aching, thinking how he could live without her for so long. He knew though she needed the time.

"I will wait for you" he brought her closer to him as he wrapped his arms around her, time slipping out of his grip.

"I love you".

· · ·

Mr Wonderful hugged her tighter. Hoping that if he held on tighter to her, he wouldn't have to leave her.

Then he kissed her gently on the forehead, and, just like that, he was gone—every sign of him. The driver had picked up his luggage.

Gabrielle sat in silence for hours. Deep, profound emptiness inside of her.

The next day she received a plane ticket to New York dated precisely six months.

"Io ti aspetto", the accompanying note said.

Tears started streaming down her face when she thought she had no more to spare. In the following weeks, Paola and Martin rallied around her and tried their best to keep her company.

But, slowly, she found herself alone, starting again.

A long time passed before she could fully comprehend why he was gone.

· · ·

"I love you ",…. she murmured into the hot embrace they were sharing, but soon she felt her hands hold on to nothingness.

She woke up and opened her eyes slowly, scared to come to a reality where he was gone.

But once she did, Gabrielle realised she was alone once again. She wrapped her arms around herself. Holding herself, trying to feel his warmth again.

"I love you!" She shouted into the empty space, hoping wherever he was, he heard her.

Days and months went by.

Gabrielle's nightmares gradually subsided, replaced by vivid, joyful memories. Slowly but surely, she had begun to find her way back to herself. And she owed that to him.

She could see now.

Gabrielle had found her inner Isadora Duncan once again and learned to channel her desire and lust for life positively for her greater good. Not just in her new creative career this time.

.   .   .

Instead of comparing now to the future or the past, she lived entirely in the present, savouring every moment.

With the death of her old self that she'd long been expecting and the birth of another, happier, higher one, Gabrielle stood erect and strong, drawing high and higher, until her stretched-out wings broke into fire.

She finally found a place to stand still, in love.

Your task is not to seek for LOVE,
but merely to seek and find all the barriers within yourself
that you have built against it
Rumi

DISCLAIMER

The Nine Live of Gabrielle: For Three She Stays is a work of fiction.

Although its form is that of a semi-autobiography (Gabrielle's) it is not one.

With the exception of public places, any resemblance to persons living or dead is coincidental. Space and time have been rearranged to suit the convenience of the book, memory has its own story to tell.

The opinions expressed are those of the characters and should not be confused with the author's.

AUTHOR'S NOTE

Thank you so much for reading *For Three She Stays*.

I hope you enjoyed this collection of novellas as escapism, but perhaps you also glimpsed something beneath as you read. A review would be much appreciated as it helps other readers discover the story.

Thanks.

If you sign up for my newsletter you'll be notified of giveaways, new releases and receive personal updates from behind the scenes of my business and books.

Go to www.thepeoplealchemist.com to get started.

Places in the book

I have set the story in real places in London and my beloved Islington. You can see some of the places here:

- Belgravia
- British Gand Prix/Silverstone
- Canonbury Square and Gardens

- Empire State Building
- London Borough of Richmond
- Wimbledon - The Championship

Bibliography

I read a lot of books as part of my research. Some of them together with other references include:

A Theory of Human Motivation - **Abraham Maslow**

Psycho-Cybernetics - **Maxwell Maltz**

Self Mastery Through Conscious Autosuggestion - **Émile Coué**

The Artist Way - **Julia Cameron**.

The Complete Reader - **Neville Goddard**, compiled and edited by **David Allen**

Tools of Titans - **Tim Ferris**

An Affair to Remember is a 1957 American romance film directed by Leo McCarey and starring Cary Grant and Deborah Kerr. It the story of two people in love who agree to reunite at the top of the Empire State Building in six months' time if they succeeded in ending their current relationships and starting new careers.
On the day of their rendezvous however, whilst hurrying to reach the place of the encounter, the woman is struck down by a car while crossing a street and is gravely injured. Meanwhile, he is waiting for her unaware of the accident. After many hours waiting, he leaves believing that she has rejected him. They reunite, of course, at the end of the movie.

Printed in Great Britain
by Amazon